This book belongs to:

....

Sometimes Mimi and her friends fly all the way to our huge
world and have lots of fun tiptoeing into toyshops and playing
hide-and-seek in the dolls' houses. Before they fly home again,
they whisper their stories to Clare and Cally,
so now YOU can hear them too!

For Scarlett and Krystal – two magical bridesmaids – Love C.B.
For Laura and Amy, with lots of love xx – C.J-I.

Hazel   Rose   Mimi   Acorn   Lily

First published 2016 by Macmillan Children's Books
an imprint of Pan Macmillan,
20 New Wharf Road, London N1 9RR
Associated companies throughout the world

www.panmacmillan.com

ISBN: 978–1–5290–1715–1
Text copyright © Clare Bevan 2016
Illustrations copyright © Cally Johnson-Isaacs 2016

The right of Clare Bevan and Cally Johnson-Isaacs to be identified as author and illustrator
of this work has been asserted by them in accordance with the Copyright, Designs and Patents Act 1988.

1 3 5 7 9 8 6 4 2

A CIP catalogue record for this book is available from the British Library.

Printed in China

mimi's magical Fairy Friends

Comet the Fairy Unicorn

by Clare Bevan and Cally Johnson-Isaacs

MACMILLAN CHILDREN'S BOOKS

The treetops were fizzing with fun!
Flags were shaking and fairies were gazing at the sky.
Everyone was waiting to see the Fairy King and Queen.

Mimi and her friends were in the tallest tree.
"I wonder what the king will be riding," said Acorn.

"I wonder what the queen will be wearing," squeaked Rose.

"Here they come!" cried Hazel.

TAN-TA-RA!

The Fairy King and Queen burst out of a
huge cloud that looked just like a fairy castle.

Down they swooped on two royal swans as big as horses.
The birds wore shiny crowns and their webbed feet swam through the air.

"Look at the little princess," giggled Mimi. "She's riding a unicorn!"

The little princess waved happily. She was sitting on her pet pony –
but today it had a sparkly spike tied to its forehead.

A band of elves played happy tunes while everyone clapped at the passing royal parade. In no time it had whirled away and the fairies flew back to their own garden.

"Let's pretend to be princesses," laughed Rose. She looked up at the cloud castle and said, "If I were a princess, I'd ride on a real unicorn."

At that moment, Mimi
saw something glitter
in the long grass . . .

"It's a box," said Hazel. "And there's a dragon carved on the lid."
The fairies tried to open the box, but it was shut tight.

But Rose said, "Ssssh!"
She held the box to her ear,
and this is what she heard:

"Slide the dragon,
    one, two, three,
Lift the lid
    and set me free."

Rose slid the dragon once, twice,
three times. She lifted the lid and . . .

out of the box flew a tiny genie!

"Thank you," he said, smiling at Rose. "You helped me escape from that horrible box, so now I'll make your favourite wish come true."

"Oh," cried Rose, closing her eyes. "I would love to ride on a real unicorn."

The genie winked.
Then he floated up, up, up and vanished like a popped bubble.

A moment later, the Genie popped back with a PING.

Beside him stood a small unicorn with twinkling wings and a golden spike.

"His name is Comet," bubbled the genie. "He's very young and he likes to eat flowers. But don't let him nibble the blue ones."

Rose hugged the unicorn and stroked his mane. "Hello Comet,"
she said shyly. Then she flapped her wings and sat on his back.
At once, they flew over the pond, past the tree house and back again.

"Hooray!" cheered the fairies.

"Thank you, Genie," called Rose. "This is my most exciting day ever! Let's all fly to the Silver River."

And away the fairies fluttered, with the genie floating after them.

Comet and Rose skimmed and soared along the Silver River
where mermaids swam . . .

high above Sparkle Park past the cloud castle,

until at last they landed in a field of flowers.

"Wait for us!" puffed the other fairies. "Our wings are tired," said Hazel with a yawn. The fairies stopped to rest and soon they all began to doze . . .

while Comet nibbled the blue flowers. Oh no!

When Rose woke up, she rubbed her eyes and saw Comet racing and chasing, prancing and dancing — while the tiny genie was trying to catch him. "I warned you about the blue flowers!" he gurgled.

"Come back, Comet!" shouted Rose. "You'll hurt yourself."
The unicorn landed with a wobble. He hiccupped. He skidded. Then . . .

PRRRANG! Comet's spike was stuck in a tree!
He pulled and he tugged, but it was no use.

"It's all my fault," Rose wailed. "I forgot about the blue flowers."
"Everyone makes mistakes," said the genie kindly. "I'm sure you'll
find a way to save your unicorn."

"Cheer up, Rose," said Mimi. "We can make a new wish to help." The fairies held hands and said:

"Sunset red and daisies white,
Show us how to put things right."

The sky started to turn rose pink, and a flock of beautiful birds with tip-tap beaks tumbled from the cloud castle and swirled around Comet's spike.

They pecked and picked at the tree.
The little unicorn jiggled and wiggled until . . .

WHOOSH! The spike shot out and Comet fell backwards, squashing a big, blue flower.

"That's a happy ending," gurgled the genie. "And just in time to take him home."

A bright star was shining as Rose gave Comet a farewell hug.
"I'll never forget you," she promised. "Not ever."

"You won't have to," whispered the tiny genie. "Fairies are good at
making wishes come true, aren't they? And everyone's allowed a
birthday wish."

Then the unicorn and the genie flew up, up, up until . . .

POP! They were gone.

Rose gazed at the star for a long time. Then she smiled.
"I'm even luckier than a princess," she told herself.
"I have a real unicorn who is just one wish away . . .

And it's my birthday tomorrow!"